Vol. 65 of the Yale Series of Younger Poets

COLLECTING EVIDENCE

BY HUGH SEIDMAN

NEW HAVEN AND LONDON, YALE UNIVERSITY PRESS, 1970

WITHDRAWN

Published with assistance from
The Mary Cady Tew Memorial Fund

Library of Congress catalog card number: 70–115377
ISBN: 0–300–01321–3 (cloth), 0–300–01322–1 (paper)

Designed by John O. C. McCrillis,
set in Times Roman type,
and printed in the United States of America by
The Carl Purington Rollins Printing-Office of
the Yale University Press, New Haven, Connecticut.

Distributed in Great Britain, Europe, and
Africa by Yale University Press Ltd., London; in
Canada by McGill-Queen's University Press, Montreal;
in Mexico by Centro Interamericano de Libros
Académicos, Mexico City; in Australasia by Australia and New
Zealand Book Co., Pty., Ltd., Artarmon, New South
Wales; in India by UBS Publishers' Distributors Pvt., Ltd.,
Delhi; in Japan by John Weatherhill, Inc., Tokyo.

Information and copyrights concerning the
original appearance of these poems are
listed in the acknowledgments.

11
e 42e

CONTENTS

ACKNOWLEDGMENTS

Acknowledgment is made to the following publications for poems which originally appeared in them:

Atlantic Monthly: "Tale of Genji"

Caterpillar: "Abstraction on His Father," "Love Poem," "Affair," "The Pillar," "Poem to Sirius," "Landscape"

Chelsea: "Constellation," "The Days: Cycle," "Pattern"

Colloquy: "Washington's Square"

Columbia Review: "The Lucencies of Last Spring" (read as the Phi Beta Kappa poem at Swarthmore College in June 1970)

Extensions: "The Modes of Vallejo Street" was originally published in *Extensions #4.*

First Issue: "Marriage," "The Sun Inside"

Intro: "The Making of Color" is from *Intro #1,* edited by R. V. Cassill. Copyright © 1968 by Bantum Books, Inc.

"The Last American Dream" is from *Intro #2,* edited by R. V. Cassill. Copyright © 1969 by Bantum Books, Inc.

Minnesota Review: "The Physicality of Desire"

New American Review: "Atavist" originally appeared in *New American Review #7.*

Poetry: "Bookstore," "Demonstration," and "Surreal Poem" originally appeared in *Poetry.* Copyright © 1969 by the Modern Poetry Association.

Silo: "Urszene," "Projection," "Minneapolis / Saint Paul," "Construction"

Sundial: "Vers Nevers," "Again," "The Reason," "The Studio," "Poem (How the Lord . . .)"

In his extraordinary study of Baudelaire, Walter Benjamin projects the image of the poet as detective, who—like the paid ferrets and informers so much a part of the scene in the Paris of his time—tirelessly explores the streets of the metropolis, scanning the behavior of the crowd for signs of its secret guilts and derelictions. Peering into the faces of the sick, the harried, the lost, Baudelaire found the clues he needed to confirm his own elusive identity. Hugh Seidman is a twentieth-century urban investigator with related characteristics. He borrows the title of his book from a passage in his sequence, "The Modes of Vallejo Street," and the phrase itself goes back to Resnais's film *Muriel,* in which boy tells girl friend why he is so busy taking pictures of Boulogne. It should be no surprise that a poet born in 1940 counts a film-maker among his literary ancestors.

Seidman became a poet after advanced study as a mathematician and physicist and after employment as a computer programmer. The "scientist of poetry" whom he addresses in one of his poems might be Einstein or Oppenheimer, but it might also be himself. When he refers to the unified field, or to "the sine curves of emotion," or to "the subtle magnet bending the signals out of shape," he does so almost casually and with an authority that we at once recognize.

> A woman consults me concerning
> her misfortune in FORTRAN.
> Her long glazed fingernail
> is polished pink & glides over
> the 132 character per line
> printer output. We examine
> her logic & sources of error.
> A scale factor is incorrect.

Her face registers the desire
I have awakened in her.
The jargon of acronyms & chance
encounters. Later we make it.

[from "The Days: Cycle"]

The impressive feature of this passage is not so much the precision of the allusion to the computer language FORTRAN as it is the ability of the poet to incorporate what he knows into a structure of feeling. "Later we make it" is the transcendent pay-off for the IBM discipline, albeit with ironic overtones. I like, too, the shock of that effortless leap from technical vocabulary to blunt vernacular.

The city that Seidman walks through is a city in ruins, like San Francisco after the earthquake or Hiroshima. Existence is marginal, as in the forms of algae, lichen, mushrooms, or as in the fibrillations of the rejected heart. His two obsessive themes are the end of love and the death of society. In "Washington's Square" he addresses the General in a voice that surely is touched with glee: "It's coming to an end George." One notes the terminal implications of his images of dread: "The teeth marks on the end/ of the rope that binds./ The wall at the edge/ of the field before fall." He can say, "This is a poem of absolute resignation." And again, "the loss of love does not cease in this world." When he produces a case-history of loss, as in "The Modes of Vallejo Street," his clinical analysis of the details of a hopeless passion proceeds irresistibly to an epiphany of desperate exaltation. He discovers the sources of his strength, the reality of his manhood, in the blaze of desire. Incidentally, is there a better account in modern literature of a lovers' quarrel than in the ninth poem of "The Modes"?

It is characteristic of Seidman that he should open his "Diary of the Revolution"—presumably based on the disturbances at Columbia University in the spring of 1968—with the observation, "He felt himself despicable. On the grass with her—." Eventually he sums up the character of his protagonist, who could occupy the post of central intelligence in almost any of his poems:

watcher of events and men
expresser of disparity
man of the inward force

> for whom everything is closed
> soldier of anger
> who is shut in solitude.

Similarly, the public event that dominates "The Last American Dream" is the burning of Newark one riotous summer; but the poet's attention is focused on a situation of personal crisis:

> and when she went away
> I turned in my sleep
> and the deepest synapse in my brain
> sparked and broke.

The poet who refuses to see himself as a hero on the stage of history, who insists, rather, on writing of defeats, incapacities, humiliations, is not perforce expressing his contempt for humanity. The self, he may be saying, is of course only a wound, a peculiarly nasty kind of psychic efflorescence, but it is at the center of a universe, and at least it is a great wound:

> Creature of the genital despair.
> Thalassal regressor.
> Stander upon the world.
> Conjoiner of the great circles.

Some of the poems have deceptive surfaces. One of my favorites, "Tale of Genji," begins with a ravishingly elegiac tone. "In Murasaki's time/ they wept at the sunsets." The life of the court and the calligraphic art of that epoch were fine, ritualized, delicate. Perspective and chiaroscuro came later, signifying a different kind of life and vision, a fracturing of the plane:

> The cold light defining shadow
> Poetry leading nowhere
>
> Occurrence made meaningless
> The injustice of history

What are we supposed to do? Weep for a golden age nearly a thousand years gone? The poet will not buy that easy sentiment. The past must not be falsified. With a stroke he shatters the glass:

Not that it mattered

Or the light
they wept at

"O rose, thou are sick!" wrote Blake at the dawn of the Industrial Revolution, and poets ever since have been studying the pathology of our society. In "Atavist" Seidman lists "the civilized diseases: gonorrhea, falling hair, bad skin, neuresthenia." Others have made similar diagnoses. But he goes a step beyond to ask a troubling question: "Is it moral to get better?" And the poem closes with an image of St. Francis kissing the leper who disdained him—that pariah who betokens all the outcasts of a system—"cursed and dragged off,/ jangling his bell on the landscape."

Like so many of the poets of his generation, as well as some of his elders, Seidman feels compelled to assume a renegade role. The air is freer and purer outside the system. Yet he seems already aware that art, as Goethe said, exists in limitations and that the creative imagination, though it adores freedom, remains irrevocably bound to a private identity, to human necessities, and to the rigors of a craft. Vessel of a rage, he seeks to master "the technique of rage." At one point he repeats the phrase, "in consummate craft and artistry," as though it were a litany. If a poem occasionally appears tighter and denser than it needs to be, we are all the more mindful that a deep violence is being contained and that the poet has been as open as he has learned to dare.

Hugh Seidman's work is alive with energizing contradictions. It combines dryness with vehemence, order with obsessiveness, knowledge with terror. This is a poet who has listened, for survival's sake, to the language of psychoanalysts, physicists, revolutionaries, statisticians, and saints; and who has made a hard vocabulary out of the mixture. The moral pressure that his imagination exerts, originates in aesthetic scruples and choices and is so evenly distributed through the syntax, the nerves and sinews, of the poem that its existence is scarcely perceptible.

One of his differences from others is in the measure and quality of his discipline, which does not find its expression in conventional modes, since it is a discipline of risks, like adventuring in space. Perhaps his education as a scientist has prepared him for dealing with the absurd. His yearning for form, his need to organize and illuminate experience, is matched by his gravitation toward chaos.

Wallace Stevens once remarked that the mind is "a violence from within that protects us from a violence without." In Seidman's version ("The Pillar") it is "the core against disturbance/ that was itself disturbance/ in its fixity and need to be."

In this disturbed and disturbing first book he makes me think of someone battering his way out of the cellar of a computer factory to prowl the streets, raging for a new life, but still tormented by desire, pursued by the old furies. Or perhaps he comes out of a gothic laboratory, where smoke-smudged alchemists, who are a breed of poet, forever seek the philosopher's stone in the glow of their alembics. If the analogy seems remote, I advise you to read the concluding poem in this collection, "The Making of Color," where color mounts on color, pigment on pigment, each in the semblance of its base ingredients, until we arrive at the extreme temperature of transubstantiation, as if the matter of the life were being converted into pure gold, pure fire, pure spiritual energy:

> The pages are stained with purple
> The letters are written in gold
> The covers are encrusted with gems
> St. Jerome remonstrates
> The curling writhes
> Molten gold on carbon
> Ink burnt ash grey
> Emerald into vapor
> The book, the codex, the manuscript
> The canvas, the panel, the wall
> Conflagrant world against world.

STANLEY KUNITZ

TALE OF GENJI

In Murasaki's time
they wept at the sunsets

It was easy

      If you were the Prince
      & in love

Calligraphy could do it

          The total life
          in the nuance of a line

& later

      The sun that had changed

The cold light defining shadow
Poetry leading nowhere

Occurrence made meaningless
The injustice of history

Not that it mattered

          Or the light
          they wept at

THE LAST AMERICAN DREAM

The black physicist knows
the distances from Newark
to precisions
of the lawns at Princeton.

In previous years
you could have seen the Great Man
or the Vassar librarian
who knew the Picassos
in Oppenheimer's house.

He wasted half his life
searching for the unified field
and when he lectured
the blackboards were shellacked
to save his chalked equations.

Scientist of poetry
they're burning Newark
and when she went away
I turned in my sleep
and the deepest synapse of my brain
sparked and broke.

WASHINGTON'S SQUARE

Here's to General Washington
who stands immobile in stone
at the base of the arch.

He sends to us
accretions from his force
& if we desire it
we may measure the precise
dimensions of the granite
& report them to the world.

In the summer the light is odd.
The men sing as we search the streets.
The air is gassed with dust.

It's coming to an end George
& I wanted to speak
as if you of all people
would know these levels.

Silent indestructible
your false teeth frozen
forever in your mouth.

FRAGMENTA

1

The sin of poetry continues
thruout the stain of his love.
Whatever I am, he thinks.
Whatever I am.

The bodies roll off
under the sickling crescent.
He moves in the moon radiance.
False light. False purity.
Whatever I am, he thinks;
It was not for these butchers.

My love. My horrid heart.
My unspeakable terrible love.
My dread and disfigurement.
My ghoul-like dreams that step
to the shrill of the reed.
Whatever I am, he thinks.
Whatever I am.

2

What do we know of that dead time,
but Yeats perhaps,
capturer of those passionate men.

You write beautiful poems,
she said, it is enough.

To believe that,
until I imagine the screams,
conjure the blood upon myself
where no blow has fallen.

3

They are the martyrs of the Word
under the nails of the lion.

We are the men of the furnace
nailed thru our skulls
in the agony of survival.

We hold to the hours
and number the lines of the dead.

We render our hands
and dream they will release us.

Our faces are our own.
We know what we may not know.

REFUSAL OF INDUCTION

Reverend R. Price
7.1.68

The soldiers dying and the starving
Bearing the Buddha on their backs

> The sheets and the pillowcases soaked with sweat
> I licked the salt from her breasts

Reich dead in jail
The bruised and abraded skin
The clearness of evil

> We prayed at five
> And at seven held vigil at Whitehall

The inquisitors had their instructions
Others had been broken
These men also knew what was to be done

MARRIAGE

For Bill and Phyllis

Went from Coast to Midwest.
Called you at three to marry me.

Rode to the airport.
The cab driver told me of *his* life.

Sobered up till seven
and saw mist float on the runway.

Flew to you in New York
and you said: No. Go Back.

Forty-five hundred miles
and your voice on the phone:
I'm not worth it. Don't cry.
You weren't my cunt anymore.

The hair at the base of my spine
is yet yours, as you said it:
Even when I don't know you.
We sat in the tub.

The sickness in me,
that I could have fought,
that I could have understood,
that for years
prevented me from loving you,
has not gone away.

The old words. The old lives.
This is a poem of absolute resignation.

BOOKSTORE

Antipodal to the will
the subversion in craft.

>I had hunted you
>in the museums.
>Days in the heat.
>The streets.

In the possible
of construction
resided release.

>Love's decibels
>louder & higher.

Someone was holding
what I thought said
the structure of rime.

>The incessance
>of leaves.

A fantasy of hair
in the tree's trunk.
The spider's
delicate stringing
but unashened.

>Not for beauty
>but that I knew.

Eyes that lay
in the obverse
of the sun.

>The endless
>transparency of night.
>Mind cut from body.
>Staring at a light
>thru yards of glass.

THE REASON

The triggered left earring
of the Gilt Bronze & Marble Negress

Made the eyes recede to show
the minute & the hour
while the right ear released
the motion of pipe organs

The furniture of Sir Charles
creditor to the English Crown

These extraordinary objects

Or Cleopatra's obelisk in the park
as we would have her: the pure form
of everything that is suspect

The conjunction of evidence

The floating of armies
& entwining arms of the corpses

An inventory of vases, porcelain,
tables & chairs, portraitures,
cabinets, painted & gilded doors,
barometers, desks

The sanctity of an age's arrogance
& I came because I wanted you

THE MODES OF VALLEJO STREET

For Laurie

San Diego, Los Angeles

1

The sailor's clothes in San Diego
where you are not
where the tide breaks the sand cliffs

I say this because I am powerless
the waves slap at me

I wade into the breakers
where the surfers take their risk
tho I
take nothing but the blows

I curse, I strike the foam
and the sea returns
the kelp and light green vines
that wrap my legs

I walk past sailors, navymen,
windows where the colors fade,
peeling cellophane
glazing ancient uniforms,
magazines of cunts and balls,
the couples
in their triggered nights

I thought of you
I thought and thought and thought of you

I rode the Greyhound here
the sun flared, the waves
snapped in the green tint windows

my hand wrapped round my cock
trying to recreate you
trying to get you back

2

In the real world I am saying
you have betrayed me because
I could not remember the bedroom

because my father is speaking
accusing me with his brutal voice

that I wish to move from him
that I covet the mysteries

the window of our room is open
and beyond: the trolley runs

and I know that my father is evil
and that this is his cruellest voice
and that this is why you have left me

3

He imagines her
a sister of her generation
passing thru Taos or the Badlands

searching in her Saab for the communes
blue eye intent on the desert

driving to an ocean
because she is no longer his

where he walks at night
in the white foam
of the spotlight on the cliff
where the lights of La Jolla lie south

where he knows
that five hundred miles from him
she will hear
the ocean that he hears

to know he is in this place
that the stars have not lied

that when he lay upon the beach
she was inside him still

that he shivered in her power
driving him
blue eye intent on the desert

4

To find the power
the sources of the power
and not this losing of her

plugging her to the past
the filament, the jeweled precision

intricate, each of us
under the summer
dreaming, delicate engines

and in his
thinking himself a robot

a boy's science fiction robot
gliding, noiseless
and the surf
audible, audible in the silence

where the armored body moved
and the robot brain
demanded their story

5

The silent radio
the dust on the unturned pages

your voice
I will no longer contemplate

writing on the walls
the rituals
after the glasses of brandy

the landscape seen from the car
here as they have foretold it in the films

dates, phrases
the bloodstained mattress
that I will not clean

since you have lain
since you have bled here
bled everywhere

I scrub the walls
I take coarse steel wool
I rub the paint to the plaster

my hands bleed
I go to the bar
I fuck with a woman

I weep in the streets
and the people glare

I wake and see your blood in the sky
and when I sleep
it is your blood in the glasses

the landscape I had forgotten was alive
the radio that I would not bear

6

You made a film of me that I have never seen
we went on the subway to shoot scenes
we went into the park in the afternoons

I lay on the ground and saw the autumn sun
the children ran around us
and the leaves whirled
and all of this was recorded

into the heart of the city
where we believed in the real
where you swore it was simple
and why did this occur

it is as distant as the sea
that I see now, unceasingly
or the numberless lives of these shores

7

When I asked for you that morning
and they said: he is lost and dying
the jailers, the kings and the queens
adorned in their disguises

and you, when the spider came
when the day tilted to its beginning
and you rose to dress
to go out into that day

the light taking you inside itself
tho I knew that you had heard

when the day tilted
when the light was like the light
I had lain in as a child
deadly thru the blinds

where I lay in the rigor
and the weight of the impending day

8

This is a story of the tar pits
the asphalt
oozing from the bowels

the smell of the highways
that lead thru hell

it is our story
for the obvious reasons

it is the true museum
surrounding the one
they have built of concrete

the tar pits
as if to speak of time
of bones that are older than men

of your bones
under your skin
of your mortality

of the scar
my finger traced
like a brand below your breasts

as I shuddered for you as if
somehow it had been mine

how I loved your body
larger than my own

and the mastadon whose pelvis
lay crushed in the tar

the old tar pits
what happens
when we are misled by appearance

it is in these public places
where the tourists come
where you, perhaps, might never come
that this is to be noted

9

He knows he must explain this
how they had eaten dinner
had eaten with others
her good friends

and how he had been angered
by the red-haired woman
and by the man that she lived with
who were *her* friends

how at that time he had told himself
he was angered by the beauty of this woman
that he, himself, could not have

but later he saw that what he hated
was the fact of their love

the love that he wanted from her
that she would not give
would not under any circumstances

so that they went to the house of these people
and he felt himself ruined
a marked man

in the light of a black and shrunken sun
that was charring him
with silence and with blame

and it came upon him
and would not relinquish him
so that the whole of the world was filled with it

and afterwards, in his house
before they took their clothes off
she yelled at him

she accused him
and he curled away from her
he let her judge him

and he claimed
that Hamlet was more than his sickness
and said this to defend himself

to save himself, instead of fighting her
instead of screaming back at her
that he was right

for finally she had said:
but I love those people
as if to say she had chosen them

and he wanted to cry, to cry out
to hold and to choke her with the knowledge
that it was he, he was the one who loved her
and not *those* people

and by what right
had she the power to choose them over him
by what right in this world
had she that power

but he could not do this
or did not know how

because clearly she had tried to want him
had tried deeply but could not
so that that was why

San Francisco, Los Angeles

10

How cold, the birds, the ducks
squawking, cawing
walking tamely on the walks
the foolish swans

across the lake the dome
the immense corinthian columns

he could see her house
a brown rectangle
high in the rows of the houses

he could understand, for the first time
why a man might turn to crime
to get what he wanted, to take by force
as one would take a woman

she had spoken of being driven to a frenzy
by a lover with bullet scars and a gun

he knew it was true, and his wish
to get a gun, to be powerful

the money to buy and sell

11

There are men
who will let the brake fluid
out of your car
or beat you to death
because someone said to

straining on the hills in second
coasting to the stop signs

the streets to your house
that account these things

I was collecting evidence
parked on the incline

shooting the picture
at some time in the afternoon
when the light was like four
sticks of dynamite under the hood

your mother painting in the skylight
or the art works scattered in the rooms

when it is impossible to free myself
from these disciplines of wealth

this poisoned needle
lodged in the upholstery

12

The wakes the boats make
and the flower of the pulsing bee

the thistle's globe and the trees
that slope to the house roofs
and the columns of the dome

the rich on these hills
and the island of Alcatraz
whose single signal
is the counter eye
revolving in your nights

it is here I relinquish you
to the tolerant bee and the waters
and to the self I have given
for wealth and your body

it is here I give you back
to the bee, the tiger dart
the seeker after sweetness

the distributer who senses
the body's warmth
of this human creature

and forfeits his flower and flies
hovering over my arms and eyes

13

To Vallejo street I came
in the summer from the place
where it is always noon
to the shadows
at the end of that street

to the colored house
of excrement and the earth
and to the objects
distributed in their orders

you went to the window and said
that you were alive
but that I was dead
you said you could not reciprocate

and your mother questioned me
and your brother said
that soon he would be married
so that then you must take packs
and depart into the mountains

and I asked if I could see you
but you said there was no time
which I could not comprehend
tho you assured me

saying that you would see me in time
in time on Vallejo street
where the dead are informed
in time, within perfect time

14

Looking from the window we saw
the dome
reconstructed of cement

sitting and speaking
smoking the cigarettes
before us on the table

in your mother's house
the museum, as you had said

and at the dome the next day
I saw the window
fixed in the tiers of the houses

it is a difference in reference
an epiphany

a certainty in the material
that I could not feel in my life

the problem
of being rich and an artist

going around the room
fingering the expensive sculpture

or you with the Black Panthers
seeking meaning, say that
seeking meaning

15

Passes the hands over the breasts
remembers the music in the earliest hours
before sleep, before the forfeit day

remembers the hunger of love and food
the images that play on the windows
and calls this the way, the necessity

the figures at night who pass
in the lighted rooms, and in the daylight

how the light must fall in the skylight
or how the figures press in the rooms at night

and the car has not moved
and the driver is motionless at his post

16

The sentry, the prisoner
the lover who is parted

Presidio, the mansions
a woman descending in the stairwells
we turn away
the last miles before the open bay

a boy crawling to the last barbed wire
a fire hydrant seared white
in the open street

I did not think of this
or I was involved with myself
when I was in your house
when I clamped my jaw

against sentiment
against the boy, outside

eighty-five men in a stifling room
one hour before dawn, the guard
rattling keys
on the bars to awaken them

17

The skeleton of the building
and the elevator climbing
in its column

half done
the one thing
he had not counted on

a cartridge belt
crossed over the chest

a man strapped to a table
with bleeding bulging feet

a lead pipe
rammed in the anus

what did it have to do with her
any of it

where
was the connection
to the animals

inches
each few thousand years
shifting thru the tar

the rivet gun marking time
on the flange of the girder

the pressure to maintain
a world that never was and her
always the one thing wrong

the one thing keeping
the building intact

half done
for which world
the leaves, the simple trees

trying to dissolve them
and they do not stop
there is nothing to make them stop

The fact that he sat
the non physical non verbal world

he said that to arise
he would have
to rearrange the discernible

more distance not needed
what he has learned
in recognition of the laws

chance not helping
tho it is written out like that

karate judo akido kendo
or get into the bedroom
and scream the sperm

on the couch she showed herself
it made him want to
make up to himself for all
who turned away

and after he wasn't in the anger
just her and the cats
below them on the floor

he felt he hadn't seen the city
but how
the sun was falling by itself

and he was late
except he had the map
and he could go

19

The empty house, the wind, the windows
and the doors banging in the drafts

the violence, the violent, the light
over the floors, the photographs of bodies
straining on the rocks, the distance
of the motion and its thought

the careful words, the violence of
we are so alone, the others who speak
in the darkened rooms, the doors
ajar in the hallways, the rumpled sheet
in the outlines of the body
the softened light, the silence

20

The failure that is his life
or, I am in hell, he thought
and so, he was

the visibility of time
when there was nothing more
they would take from him

it was all for a mood, a travesty
a woman turning in the sunlight
it was what was expected

the rats that no one had noticed
a rebuttal of form, a remark
that sweat is uncomfortable

21

And if it is to end this way
by the sea
to mean that it begins

in the chill before the winter
before the spring will come again
to unmesh him

as he lay under the sun and slept
until waking at six he saw
the beach, empty, and felt afraid

away from friends, from her
a man
stripped bare and walking to the water

to leave his life behind him
when there is only this to be unsaid

New York

22

Those photographs of fucking in all its forms
the young women as if ageless in
the eternity of their bodies

he was weakened in an abject insatiable desire
as the dwarf
came swinging on his crutches

the useless legs arcing in half circles
but someone
would want him, the miracle

and the birds there
pecking after seeds, greedy, gobbling

23

The way you would see them
ranged on the mountain and then in motion
garlanded, beribboned

the women and the men together
over again, yet different
passing in the world's frame, for themselves
for the days again

the beauty of one's own name
not out of economies
but the path they take, as they come

into the sight of the cities
our lives to undo them

garlanded, beribboned in the old way
the female children alive, and the male children
each to have pleasure

24

Coming from this, to be conscious
in the parks, in the buildings
a mind among only its own things

whatever I can use, at the wedding
their fatality appeared, the women

her body in the ivory dress
as she sat and I stood apart from her
behind her, before the bride and groom

but to have taken her hand
to have dragged her before the altar
we were the ones—marry us

25

It is all energy
too much to dissipate

the freedom that he cannot use
clamps down
does not allow the resource out

and backwards, that tangible past
when he did not see
what a man must decide

but he would go among these people
because it was his life
to say to her
become what you are or die

to break past the curtains to their parts
unclothe their bodies
and walk within this wedding
this marriage in the feast of marriages

ONE OF US

the man in the wheel chair not quite dead
trying to hang on, to be lucid
like poor sick Freud who would take no drug

but it was going, or was gone
the way all the phones were dead in the subway
or like the next day, when the toilet broke

how any attempt made him feel profane
how he thought to walk naked in the streets

the point where the needle spiked his arm
when the doctor spoke the secret in his ear
and his fingers uncurled to nothing

his torso trembling, so horny on the bed
bearing down and remembering

and the clarity before confusion
came to cloud his heart again

BLIND   DUMB

My father wrestled me
I bathed with him naked

I saw her naked breast
My breath left me

                    I gasped for air

He said to

        BREATHE

He hit me in the ribs
BREATHE

When she turned her naked breast to me

            DUMB and BLIND

ABSTRACTION ON HIS FATHER

The fire doors
open out going down
hinged at the left
to the outside frame.

In the intricacy of the stacks
tier on tier
turning always right

            it was possible
            for a man
            to remain unnoticed.

incurved
the frame's vault
the door's metal
the hand opens
in the gesture
of closing

There is the instance
of the fire door
locked to rescind
the forces of heat

            slammed full
            to the cores
            of memory

            & the artless rest
            to him who desires.

PENTAD

He dreamed in the morning of M.
Not in her own form but in L's.
Love in its first intention.
The difference was five years.
He awoke like a man in prison.
The window shade was translucent.
That day, in the dream's time,
he had sat with her in silence.
There had been three others.
She was the fifth,
but did not think of him.
He walked into the autumn.
He fought to remember.

AGAIN

the humiliation of the feeling
that he gave it
the memory and the actual
his hand covered with semen
typing in the dark by touch
the code he will never understand
not the thin hips of the gentile
but the ass of the Jewess
the technique of rage
her smell as he lowered his face

THE PHYSICALITY OF DESIRE

1

There is a photograph of a starving child
on the white wall of the room.
Its belly is distended and balloon-like.
Its hands are crossed over its face
as if it were crying in a great despair.
The picture upsets her.
I have ceased to notice him,
but I say it is to remind me of the world.
We sleep in each other's arms.
Perhaps she dreams I am the boy.

2

I am in a bathroom on my knees
bending over a toilet.
A man and a woman are bathing.
I am intent on forcing
banana skins and faeces
down the mouth of the urinal.
Each time I try I fail,
and I must begin the cycle again.

3

Nothing in the mind but darkness.
They ask me what I feel.
I say: nothing.
They say: he is lying.
I turn on the bed. I think of a woman
possessed of an infinite tenderness.
We are at the sea. She is saying:
this is the virtue of the hour of
unending elaboration.

ATAVIST

Venturing to the world:
the doctor's office.

The civilized diseases:
gonorrhea, falling hair,
bad skin, neurasthenia.

Body edging into spirit
and I debate:
Is it moral to get better?

St. Francis kissed that leper,
who disdained him,
cursed and dragged off,
jangling his bell on the landscape.

LOVE POEM

surcease
surcease

the cloud's edge
a crack
in the sun's face

surcease
surcease

the church tower
dead east
in the mornings

brown hair tied with a black felt ribbon

a building with the windows gone

men throwing boards from a truck

as thus:

from the mind's light
as I lay
insane with love of you
the spider
descended on a thread
again
to bind me into death

LESSON PLAN

Get to the museum to see:
Renoir and Mallarmé in Berthe Morisot's salon
posing at a mirror

The Pennsylvania Artillery, Battery B
an officer with drawn sword and the cannons
men—gazing and shooting

Daguerreotypes of women
The Boston Beauty by Southworth and Hawes

The rubble of the San Francisco earthquake
faded and engraved on platinum paper

And then get out into the park to watch
two men who come to open a man hole:
staring in on their knees and arguing
until one gets up to dig in the inside

Schoolgirls sketching trees
and there's no way out of any of it

DEMONSTRATION

The loudspeaker repeating the same message
The children running on the grass
The people & the precise hexagons of the cobbles

From high up on the wall
Everything takes this quality of measure
The action of falling apart & together

It is a new thing with us
The game of death on the squares of this board
The calculation of moves & counters

The sleek cat on the ledge curled to an oblong
The bus noise & the park & the towers of the city
Or—We have known this before but differently

DIARY OF THE REVOLUTION

4.23.68

He felt himself despicable.
On the grass with her—
To beg her to help him.

The books under his arm.
The wind over cold earth.

It was a spring afternoon,
but still he did not understand.

4.24.68

Barricaded at doors. Siren. Gate locked.
Police circling buildings.
The body desire of sexual communion.

Continuing night in the night of sleep.
Rain falling ceaselessly.
World dream, solitude, deepening, unreachable.

In the tunnel, crawling, hands feeling a wall.

Deadness in the groin.
Arms around a man's neck.
Plunging a knife into neck cords.
Who will not bleed, nor die.

The electric bulb of a room in childhood.

4.25.68

The emotional plague
Reich said

He said it and they murdered him
It was as simple as that

And who even now believes it
Inside or out

4.26.68

The impossible realized
The madness accepted as his own

After the night's vigil
Climbed into sunlight

She chose a flower and gave it
They walked the park at dawn

Green hill and the white
Cylindrical oil tank

Stared over water to the world
Slept the day till nightfall

4.27.68

The light . . .

They sat on the steps in it
her arms around him

Their moment past

One could have said
they were kind to each other

●

The nostalgia of a life
too far off to be considered.
A tree consoles us, a squirrel, a poem.
We are pierced with a momentary memory.
We weep, beat on the bed, fall exhausted;
borne on the slough and crest of the wave.

●

Together they wake and sleep,
break bread, partake of the sun

Together in calamity

And he is sick with it
rooted and rotted

4.28.68

thrust of counter force
rising against death in the genitals
engine of charge discharge

watcher of events and men
expresser of disparity
man of the inward force

for whom everything is closed
soldier of anger
who is shut in solitude

cruelty and hell of the mind
one person in the world
driven off by him

watcher
strengthener of hatred
what is there where love is not

AFFAIR

The black pigeon straggles under the parked car
I feel the pain of the cracked wings
I reach to it but it hides near the wheel

Later I see the bloody and headless
Half-body of a pigeon lying in the street

The ease of such comparison persists
We struggle to survive these sentiments

THE PILLAR

Strange how the sense
adhered to form significance
and called it to assume itself.

The immaculate pillar
of their self-destructed winter
glinted whitely in the mind.

The fault was to think
she would be anywhere—
an imperfect attention
which informed each act
in a structure of error.

He felt he could feel differently:
in perfect attention
the use of event must follow.

But when the word passed,
and perception closed
to its distorted spore,
he faltered to the sense
of what was lost from sense.

Yet the pillar stood
thru all humiliation and mischance,
the core against disturbance
that was itself disturbance,
in its fixity and need to be.

For love to make his way
to this whitened pillar
demanding its solidity.

THE DAYS : CYCLE

Black Saturday bubbles up &
Peace Eye Bookstore is closed.
In the park mamas & kids
pass time at the benches.
Flat-chested copper-haired girl
consoles her son. For a second
I think she's speaking to me.
No wedding ring. Kids & ex-husband
stare thru her face & dare me.
I go back to Avenue A.
Peace Eye is still shut tight.

•

A woman consults me concerning
her misfortune in FORTRAN.
Her long glazed fingernail
is polished pink & glides over
the 132 character per line
printer output. We examine
her logic & sources of error.
A scale factor is incorrect.
Her face registers the desire
I have awakened in her.
The jargon of acronyms & chance
encounters. Later we make it.

•

Boredom, revolutions, money,
& love. Human dignity.
The stars wheel overhead.
Newton believed them fixed
altho now we are wiser.

A woman put me down & Freud
smoked twenty cigars a day.
My friend spoke of prophets
& profit. The air conditioner
makes the only living sound.

●

If the flowers blacken & the sun
is unending? Delicate pastels & perfume.
Letters on the thinnest papers.
To the watcher: This is to inform you
I am alive & content amid the acreage
& private ruins. The mirrors
contrive to enamour me of distance.
The gold millimeter encircles my finger.
I have feared that pain would pass
& have known that endurance would robe me.
Perforce & perforce.

●

Her lingering finger smell &
Saturday afternoon I walk,
buy a cigar, & read in the bar.
We lie & the wind blows in
from the garden she asks of
& if the maple & the oak
are beautiful in the fall.
The ageless stars that hold us
by the force which is our own.
The laws of God & those
who are beyond the forms.
Hilarious to see my face
in the face I try not to see.

THE STUDIO

the breaking waves

                      & the earth
floating in the space of lunar seas
photographs of water
convulsion   reciprocity

spume thrown on sides
of clear plastic cubes
droplets of glycerine
as if water had condensed

the upper arms & body
like a man's
tools hung on pegboard
breasts belying strength

carpenter
plunge & drip in the seas

& over us
           like a world
another's nakedness
one who had removed herself

dancer

the carnate sea
the scene from Hampton's rocks
the secret of sound

                    glycerine

the insects that inhabit amber

we came to streets
stood & passed beneath
glass globes of light
                    concrete

Picasso head on gravel

our bodies remember
the waking pain

our bodies remember her silence
the power inside her
                        the fear
that sent her nude to Bellevue

we saw in the film
the couple copulating
female top up
bobbing to the rhythm of music

at the farthest touch of the wave
at the maze of fatigue

                        Edgerton's
strobe photo crown of
a milk drop's splash

two women
            burst to the conscious
life of the water world
art's face
            wash over us
more real than water

URSZENE

The same sleep in each bed
Silence & the currents of the ganglia

Wetness of the wood
Fungus ingrained with blood
Explosion caverning underworlds
Cythonic figure—whose eyes
Are the variegate of mushroom

Voices in the room he is absent from
His face alive in the blackness
Who needs so much and may ask for nothing

POEM

How the Lord of Death came to lay his moist finger at my throat
I went to the fork of the streets
But the distances were different and had lengthened
I heard the voices behind me as I ran
And awoke to the leaves which were the wind
Insane with tiredness and distant from myself
And how I had awakened beside you years ago
To fend away your touch turning in half sleep
For the loss of love does not cease in this world

THE LUCENCIES OF LAST SPRING

1

In reverse of ritual
the fish are returned
buried in the great ditches

precise as the atoms at Japan
where the red tuna is caught and eaten raw
the sea bass, shrimp and squid

in the rain
in the smouldering of water
at the scale's high end

these millions of experiments
in the sciences of time

2

Two dancers dance in the white light of their bodies
two dancers strobe photographed
in the flow of motion to the frozen form

the translucent segments of a worm
collapsed thru each other

talking of it
sitting in the air-conditioned silence
staring thru the sheets of glass
sipping coffee

speaking easily of the future
as if the future were real and each of us
had within himself, a part of it

3

Stop rhythm
the growths of imagination
the wish to be there and here
in the fury world

the mushroom
the blank negative energy of white rice
bread and sugar

clogging their stomachs with negation
they say harvest the sea
the gardens of algae and lichen

but their bodies are black with negation
and will never allow the green of those oceans

4

Nerve gas and acid
the frantic heart
caged in the chest of stone
the filling of the arteries
with the micrograms of waste

he had said that spring
was the season he hated

and that Hitler was a psychopath
who had killed in the spring

it was understandable

the face of death
that he has never seen
which he sees
in the changing water

as her face had changed
under his eyes and had passed
thru every stage of himself
to its final transfiguration

5

And if he cheats, and if he says
that each step
is like a station of the cross

the people positioned
under the dome and the sky
like men
on the tiers of their pyramids

that will allow him nothing
but the tears
refilling in the folds of his eyes

as the breath departs
and the lungs release their air

6

The foetus staring
wrapped in the transparent
glowing placenta

the red-haired girl he met
in the morning

the belief that everything
was a failure of passion

flat out at the sun
the perfection of vowels

this rope
to suspend the world
that turns us upon ourselves

7

Grey canvas painted in
in pain, in death
in simplicity

a pitiless world, remorseless
a world without error
blank, perfect as stone

and aside
from the pressure of bare breasts under silk

it was meaningful to reach the point
where risk was not meaningful
and then, to take it even then

8

Spring rain, the reigning spring

two people speak for hours after parting
bodies and hands
to take hold within compassion

John Cage on pain:
neither too much nor too little
but enough

once mushrooms almost killed him
tho he is an expert

thus possibly
the danger of so much chance
but don't question what is past question

9

Borne of the human bone and witless
no shape, every shape
nothing to elude

in consummate craft
in consummate craft and artistry

each grief, each relief
each day and every day
in consummate craft and artistry

VERS NEVERS

For the film "Hiroshima Mon Amour"

1

Dusk in the north of France.
Sick from tasting. Tree-lined
isolate roads. The farmhouse,
the church tower, the open field.

The cobbled streets of towns.
Houses close on the cobbles.
Strong rain. A solitary figure
turning behind a wall.

2

I, in the mask of physicist, leave Paris bearing a pack, hitch-hiking
south with a French couple on vacation. We drive in a large black
car. The wheel is at the left as it is in America. I go to Nevers
because of the heroine of *Hiroshima:* the eternal nurse and god-
dess. They say: *Vous êtes un physicien très sentimental.*

3

Peaches in Nevers
Two women in black
Clouds mirrored on water
A fisherman on a chair in a boat

The park's war monument:
Tears on the woman's face
Grooves in the bronze

63

4

We know how the seven tributaries of the Ota drain and fill
And when the sun hemorrhaged on Peace Square
How the shadows were indured on stone
We know how the light of the Loire enumerates Nevers

5

In the black hole
Alone in the black hole

To speak of it
The blackness of the hole

Cratered earth
Sand blasted to glass

Vaporized ear lobe
Erogeny that is lost

Shocked from the relative
The absolute increment

Standard clock's
Unvarying seconds

The weight of death
The change of the light

PATTERN

Why this lust
when there is nothing mutable
but the hope of change
in the mind that knows this.

Muscles anchored to negation.
Interminable days
in the intervals of our receivers.
The sine curves of emotion.

She left me with distortion.
She said this is where you are
and what can I do.
The subtle magnet
bending the signals out of shape.

PROJECTION

walks any street
until a face appears
the unmistakable beauty
who makes no sign

        a phone call is made
        imbued with complexity
        a life at its end
        in detached phrases

the wetness
of the inside
the open eye
the broken point
of the hardness

        when the pieces meshed
        and the sun appeared
        to mark a clarity
        he had brought to being

someone he had sought
in the dream

        the earth man
        striving to awaken
        in the world of men

tiered on the slopes
of the park
their shirts off
and the women
the touchable source

        the couples
        watching him
        as he walked
        the stone path

MINNEAPOLIS / SAINT PAUL

1

when he settled
into that plane

>   sphere window
>   shell's hold

and for an instant
felt how it felt

>   to fall
>   thru a certain eternity

fought back by thought
a mind state

>   lights
>   engine's outwardness

2

You could have seen him
that being, that 'he'
the son at the airport
with his parents
in his suit, finally
to live apart from them

He lay those mornings
in the warmth of the gas heater
under the grey cube of the skylight
the diffusion
the first flowering awareness

The city : 500 miles from
anything in any direction

He wanted to set it as chronology
he felt the pain as an emblem
she, and no other, would know him

3

How can he summon that past to say
This is why I am so awkward
Why, when you ask me to speak, I cannot

He thinks of it as a childhood
Immense and distant

The bad noise, the back ground
The signals hanging on the air waves

4

Summit Avenue's houses
the houses on River Road
the path over the docks
the dark barges
the foaming water
the night shields him
drunk in the old grievances
the bars of Seven Corners
the aftermath of anger

                    night comes again
          he walks on University Avenue
                              he crosses the Tenth Avenue Bridge
          the red city of
          one glaring neon
                              contained
                                        isolate
the black smoke on the black sky
                    the grain elevators on the tracks
    The Great Northern Railway
              the desolations of Northfield
                        Pillsbury's daughters on the continent
          continuant then
                        and then her

5

Drifting in over
the strung beacons

The ideal of
transparence

Clogged ears
perceive music

At first afraid
in the fuselage

Breathing and
taking note

The vapor trails where
he has been

CONSTRUCTION

The joint of two stone slabs
Extends his spine toward sky.
His fist draws round an iron rail.
The city lies south.

Her body at concurrence of
Perpendicular triangle arms.
Two bridges cross the river.

Lumen of the city. Torpor.
The insect fear that crept into his form.
Filtered light thru centuries of water.

Concrescence.

So much that is malleable. So much that is
Unchangeable.
Waking for six years
Holding her name.
                    Occurrence that
Caused him to know morality.

POEM TO SIRIUS

Pathfinder.
Opener of the ways.
Guardian of the horizon.
Bringer forth and destroyer.

In the night of enlightenment.

To stare at the putrid dog
until we ourselves are the stench.

Keeper of the word.
Dealer of the logos.

—I am the path to possession.

The teeth marks on the end
of the rope that binds.

The wall at the edge
of the field before fall.

LANDSCAPE

I thought how once the sun rose,
and of the black sun,
hung forever in this heaven.

I lean my arms on the balustrade,
face to the sea and form you:
the vanish point of the dead horizon.

At level to the topmost branch,
the total length of the tree,
pivoting slowly to the wind.

Creature of the genital despair.
Thalassal regressor.
Stander upon the world.
Conjoiner of the great circles.

THE SUN INSIDE

He reads the poets
and sees the sun
and thinks: in another
part of the city
it will be different.

So: he gets the express
and goes downtown,
fast, he times it.

In the bookstore reads:
yellow is the fatal color,
Van Gogh and Kandinsky
for instance, the probable
danger to the soul.

Confirmed premonition
of the sidewalks.

Lover of pride: be
careful of the days,
as they, who have
prayed for you.

SURREAL POEM

Everyone went away and I
said 'white', which I learn today, is
the color of death; and the girls
in the dress store, dressed in satin-
like synthetic, before the mirrors,
are still themselves. What else is there,
this falling into ourselves, as
thru the bathtub water, covered
with the film of mercury.

THE MAKING OF COLOR

White

Parchment and paper left clean
or the lead, called white, or ceruse

The stack of vinegar and lead
embedded in tanbark or dung;
the temperature of fermentation,
moisture, carbon dioxide,
and the acid vapor of vinegar—
until a crust is formed on the coils of metal:
the white carbonate and hydroxide of lead

The metal may be wrapped in marc,
the refuse of grapes from the wine press,
or else in the waste from beer

The fundamental character is density,
opacity, and brilliant whiteness

Those who work this are warned of
the poisonous dust of this residue—
retained in the human system as
the body's tolerance incurably declines

There is the white of bone,
or of egg shell, or of oyster,
calcined and powdered,
or a pigment of chalk
to be mixed with orpiment

Black

Certain insects sting in oak
nodules called galls from which

tannic and gallic acids are soaked

Mixed with a salt of iron
to form a purple-black liquid
that blackens with age

The color of iron-inks
oxidized in the fibers
of parchment and paper

incaustum – burnt in

or less frequently
suspensions of graphite
or of lampblack

Red

Minium in the sense of cinnabar
the native red sulphide of mercury

Pliny reports
the excellent mines are in Spain
the property of the State

Forbidden to break up or refine
but sent under seal to Rome

Ten thousand pounds per year
the price sustained by law
seventy sesterces a pound

Liver-colored or occasionally scarlet
but a bright red when ground

Blue

Cloth dyed blue
licensed by the Crown

Ultramarine – lapis lazuli
pounded in a bronze mortar
Cennino relates

Eight ducats an ounce
for the patrons to purchase

Purple

The color of cheeks and the sea
Purpureus – the porphyry
The shellfish or the whelk
The murex – the purples of antiquity
Porphyrygenetos – born to the purple
A single drop from a skeleton

The stripes of the Roman togas
The purple of the ancient courts
The purple of Byzantium   The purple
of the great codices written in gold
The purple ink of the Patriarch
in the letters to the Pope of Rome

Parchment dyed shellfish-purple
crimson, plum-color, black
and the true purple – rivaling gold

Gold

Sheet metal, foil the thickness of paper,
leaf that is thinner than tissue

Malleable but difficult to powder

Sawed or filed into coarse particles
ground with honey or salt and washed

Hardened with a base metal
filed and crushed and retrieved in acid

Brittle amalgams which are ground
mercury driven off by heat

The goldbeaters place a thin square
at the center of parchment and over this

more parchment and metal – hammered
until the gold spreads to the edges—
cut and the process repeated—
for the finest leaf, a sheet
of ox intestines – goldbeater's skin

One hundred and forty-five leaves
beaten from a ducat
Venetian – fifty-four troy grains

Powdered gold in suspension
chrysography
              letters
on the reds and purples and blacks
of purple-dyed parchment
polished with a smooth hard stone
or with a tooth
                 the appearance
of filings of metallic gold

Fire

The pages are stained with purple
The letters are written in gold
The covers are encrusted with gems
St. Jerome remonstrates
The curling writhes
Molten gold on carbon
Ink burnt ash grey
Emerald into vapor
The book, the codex, the manuscript
The canvas, the panel, the wall
Conflagrant world against world